KT-417-798

This is one of a series of books specially prepared for very young children.

The simple text tells the story of each picture and the bright, colourful illustrations will promote lively discussion between child and adult.

British Library Cataloguing in Publication Data

Hurt, Mary
    Looking at animals. — (Ladybird Toddler books.
    Series no. 833;6)
    1. Animals — Juvenile literature
    I. Title
    591   QL49
    ISBN 0-7214-0787-0

Published by Ladybird Books Ltd Loughborough Leicestershire UK
Ladybird Books Inc Auburn Maine 04210 USA

© LADYBIRD BOOKS LTD MCMLXXXV
All rights reserved. No part of this publication may be reproduced, stored in a retrieval system, or transmitted in any form or by any means, electronic, mechanical, photo-copying, recording or otherwise, without the prior consent of the copyright owner.

Printed in England (3)

Ladybird Toddler Books

looking at animals

written by MARY HURT
illustrated by PAT OAKLEY *of* HURLSTON DESIGN

Ladybird Books

It's a sunny day.
Let's go and look
   at the animals.
There will be lots to see.

Here are the elephants.
They are so big.
Look at their trunks and white tusks.
See their big ears!

The elephants are keeping cool.
They can squirt water from their trunks.
Doesn't this look fun?

The chimpanzees make us laugh.
They can do funny tricks.
Which chimpanzee do you like best?

These monkeys are swinging in
the branches.
The baby monkey is eating a banana.

The big lions are sleepy.
They have just eaten some meat for
    their dinner.
We mustn't wake them up.

These little lion cubs are enjoying
a game in the sunshine.
They love to play; just like you.

Polar bears have lots of soft fur.
It keeps them warm in the cold water.
Can you see the baby bear up
   on the rocks?
Be careful, baby bear!

The giraffes are very tall.
What long legs
   and long necks!
They can reach the leaves from the
   tops of the trees.

A keeper is bringing fish for
the sea-lions.
They are very hungry.
They make a lot of noise.

The penguins smell fish.
They run to a keeper for their dinner.
Which penguin is eating a fish?

The hippopotamuses like to lie in
 the water.
It keeps them cool.
Is one hippopotamus yawning?
What enormous teeth!

Here come the ostriches.
They are big birds
   with long legs.
They can run very fast
   but they cannot fly.

Two crocodiles are on the bank.
How many are in the water?
Watch out!
They have lots of sharp teeth!

See the slithery snakes.
What beautiful colours!
Which one do you like best?

Here are the zebras.
Look at their stripes.
Which zebras are eating grass?
Which one is the baby?

The tiger cubs are having
a game with their mother.
They are having fun.

Here are the camels.
They have just had some dinner.
They look very pleased with themselves.

The kangaroos have
   long back legs.
They are good at jumping.
Can you see the baby in its
   mummy's pouch?

Here are some animals that are
  safe to touch.
Can you see rabbits and hamsters;
  lambs and a calf;
  kittens and puppies;
  and goats and donkeys?
Which is your favourite animal?